Welcome to ALADDIN QUIX!

If you are looking for fast, fun-to-read stories with colorful characters, lots of kid-friendly humor, easy-to-follow action, entertaining story lines, and lively illustrations, then **ALADDIN QUIX** is for you!

But wait, there's more!

If you're also looking for stories with tables of contents; word lists; about-the-book questions; 64, 80, or 96 pages; short chapters; short paragraphs; and large fonts, then **ALADDIN QUIX** is *definitely* for you!

ALADDIN QUIX: The next step between ready to reads and longer, more challenging chapter books, for readers five to eight years old.

Read more Aladdin QUIX books!

Read all the Mini Mermaid Tales
#1 *The Friendship Wish*
#2 *The Dolphin Dream*
#3 *The Princess Promise*

Read ROYAL SWEETS
by Helen Perelman
#1 *A Royal Rescue*
#2 *Sugar Secrets*
#3 *Stolen Jewels*
#4 *The Marshmallow Ghost*
#5 *Chocolate Challenge*

Read LITTLE GODDESS GIRLS
by Joan Holub and Suzanne Williams
#1 *Athena & the Magic Land*
#2 *Persephone & the Giant Flowers*
#3 *Aphrodite & the Gold Apple*
#4 *Artemis & the Awesome Animals*
#5 *Athena & the Island Enchantress*
#6 *Persephone & the Evil King*
#7 *Aphrodite & the Magical Box*
#8 *Artemis & the Wishing Kitten*
#9 *Athena & the Mermaid's Pearl*
#10 *Persephone & the Unicorn's Ruby*
#11 *Aphrodite & the Dragon's Emerald*
#12 *Artemis & the Dog's Diamond*

Mini Mermaid Tales
by Debbie Dadey

The Princess Promise

Illustrated by
Fuuji Takashi

ALADDIN QUIX
New York London Toronto Sydney New Delhi

This book is a work of fiction. Any references to historical events, real people, or real places are used fictitiously. Other names, characters, places, and events are products of the author's imagination, and any resemblance to actual events or places or persons, living or dead, is entirely coincidental.

ALADDIN QUIX
Simon & Schuster Children's Publishing Division
1230 Avenue of the Americas, New York, New York 10020
First Aladdin QUIX hardcover edition October 2024
Text copyright © 2024 by Debbie Dadey
Illustrations copyright © 2024 by Fuuji Takashi
Also available in an Aladdin QUIX paperback edition.
All rights reserved, including the right of reproduction in whole or in part in any form.
ALADDIN and the related marks and colophon are trademarks of Simon & Schuster, LLC.
Simon & Schuster: Celebrating 100 Years of Publishing in 2024
For information about special discounts for bulk purchases, please contact Simon & Schuster Special Sales at 1-866-506-1949 or business@simonandschuster.com.
The Simon & Schuster Speakers Bureau can bring authors to your live event. For more information or to book an event contact the Simon & Schuster Speakers Bureau at 1-866-248-3049 or visit our website at www.simonspeakers.com.
Jacket designed by Karin Paprocki and Ginny Chu
Interior designed by Mike Rosamilia
The illustrations for this book were rendered digitally.
The text of this book was set in Archer Medium.
Manufactured in the United States of America 0824 LAK
2 4 6 8 10 9 7 5 3 1
Library of Congress Control Number 2024010391
9781534489370 (hc)
9781534489363 (pbk)
9781534489387 (ebook)

To Alex

Cast of Characters

Poppy: Mergirl who is looking for the princess

Aunt Bella: Poppy's aunt

Mrs. Fangtooth: Poppy's neighbor

Sam: Poppy's younger brother

Shelly: Mergirl playing in the mud

Aqua: Poppy's friend

Freddie: Poppy's friend

Rosie: Poppy's friend

Contents

Chapter 1: Meet Poppy — 1

Chapter 2: Mud Pies — 8

Chapter 3: Are You a Princess? — 19

Chapter 4: Princess in the Park — 35

Chapter 5: Biggest and Best — 41

Word List — 49

Questions — 52

Meet Poppy

"Maybe just one more," **Poppy** said. She plucked a sea lily from the ocean floor and added it to the pretty **bouquet** in her hand.

"How lovely," **Aunt Bella** said from her seat on the porch.

"Pretty enough for a princess," their **neighbor, Mrs. Fangtooth**, told them. "Did you know that a princess lives in our city?"

"Really?" Poppy asked.

Mrs. Fangtooth nodded. "Yes, she's an **enchanting** young lady. Although sometimes she is a bit too noisy. I just saw her in the park on my way home from the library." Mrs. Fangtooth worked at the Trident City Library.

"May I go to the park, Aunt Bella?" Poppy asked, thinking it would be exciting to meet a princess. One of Poppy's books showed a princess wearing a

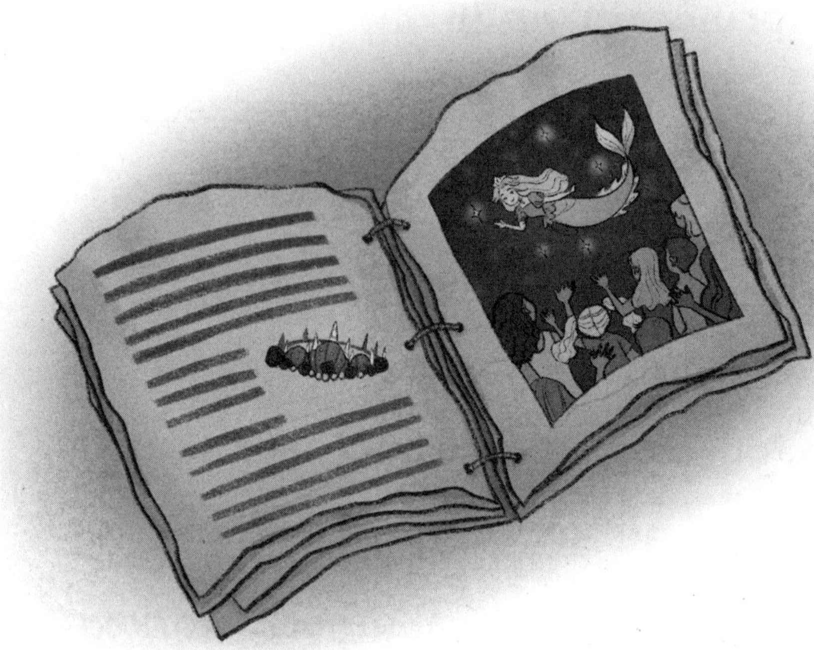

crown and waving to a **crowd**. Her fancy gown sparkled with jewels. She even had sparkles on her tail.

What would it be like to be a

princess? Surely everyone would be nice. Princesses could have candy for breakfast, lunch, and even dinner if they wanted! How fun would that be?

Aunt Bella tapped her chin with her green tail. Poppy wished she was more like her aunt. Lots of merpeople had green tails. No one had a bright yellow tail with strange swirls like Poppy's!

"Here, these are for you." Poppy pushed her bouquet into her aunt's hands.

"All right, you may go," Aunt Bella said. "But you must stay where I can see you."

Poppy grinned. That was easy. Their house was across the street from the park. Aunt Bella lived with Poppy, her mom, and **Sam**, Poppy's little brother.

"But...," Aunt Bella added.

Uh-oh! Poppy didn't like it when her aunt said "but." It usually meant something bad.

"You must take Sam with you," Aunt Bella said.

Oh no! That *was* bad. She liked her brother, but he liked nothing more than to get dirty, and he especially loved playing in the mud. Messy, yucky, not-princess-like mud.

"Do I have to?" Poppy asked.

"Yes, you do," Aunt Bella told her.

Poppy nodded. It wouldn't be easy finding a princess with a muddy little merboy tagging along. But that was exactly what she was going to do. No matter what!

Mud Pies

Just as Poppy had **suspected**, Sam went right to the biggest mud puddle in the park. *Splat!* He plopped down and moved his tail back and forth. Soon he was **coated** with slime.

"**Ugh!**" Poppy said. Why had Aunt Bella made her bring Sam today?

"Please make mud pies with me?" Sam asked. His three-year-old face looked so sweet that Poppy was **tempted**. After all, they made him so happy. They also made him very icky!

"You look like a mud pie yourself," Poppy said with a giggle. Her brother was a mess! He even had muck on the top of his head. How had that happened?

"Please, Poppy, please!" Sam pleaded.

"Sam, I don't want to get dirty," Poppy told him, folding her arms over her tummy. What if she actually did meet the princess? She didn't want to look like a wreck.

"I'll make mud pies with you," a mergirl who sat nearby said with a smile. She looked older than Poppy and had long red hair. Her clothes were already dirty, just like Sam's.

Sam grinned. "**Yay!** Look how mushy gushy it is."

The mergirl laughed. It *was* mushy gushy. The gunk also dripped down Sam's arm. He squeezed the blob in his hand, and mud **squirted** onto his face.

"**Sam!**" Poppy cried. "Don't get that in your eyes. It'll hurt!"

"Don't worry, Poppy," he said.

The red-haired mergirl **plunked** down beside Sam and began making slimy pies. "By the way, I'm **Shelly**. And I have an idea for what we can make next."

Poppy floated a little away, trying to stay clear of the mess. She looked around at the crowded park. Merpeople sat on benches talking. Merkids played shell ball. Poppy smiled at some of her merfriends on the swings. Families passed Poppy, Shelly, and Sam on their way out of the park. Where could the princess be?

"Hi, Poppy!" Her merfriend **Aqua** swam over from the swing set. Two other merfriends, **Freddie**

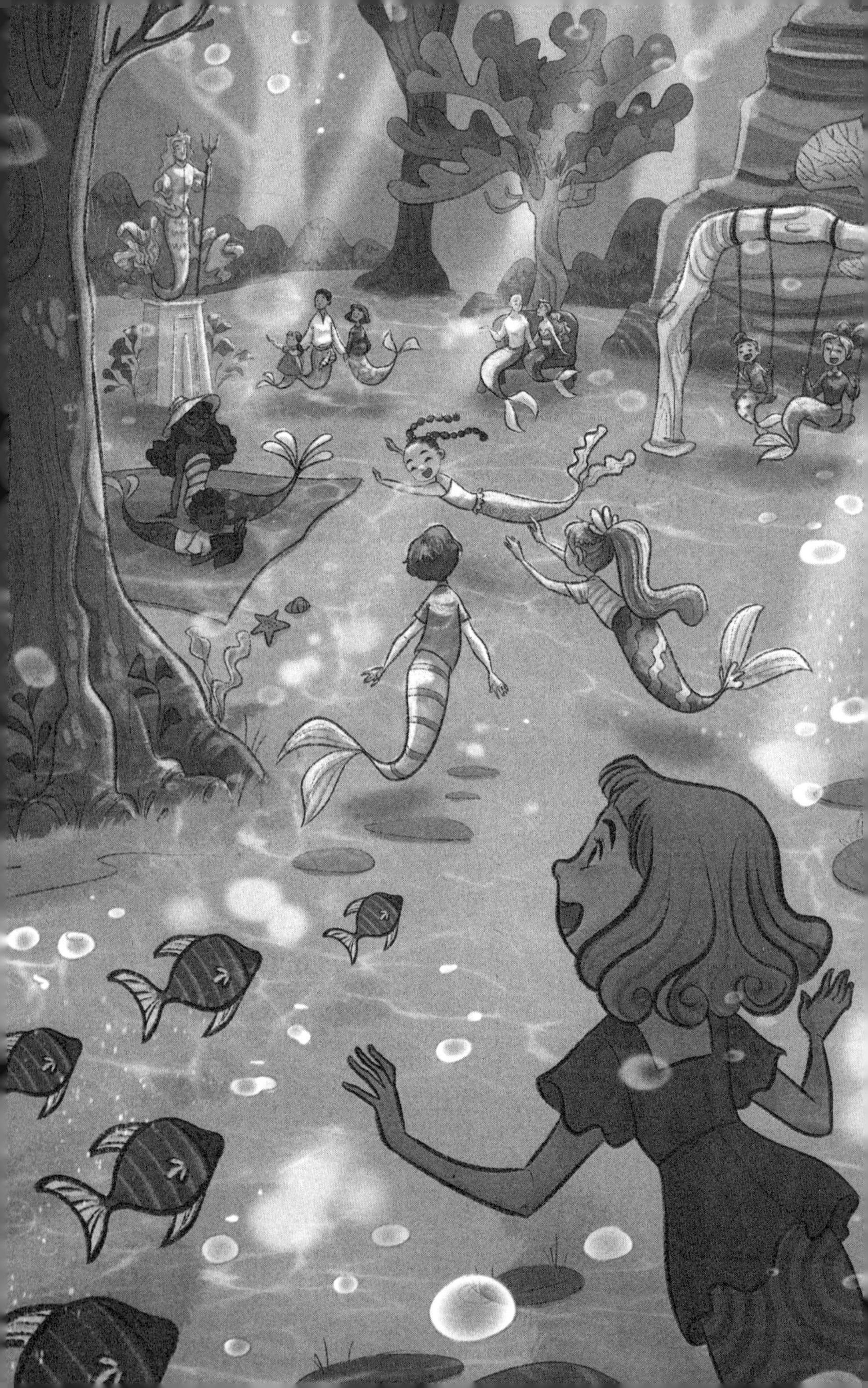

and **Rosie**, swam up beside her. "Come swing with us?"

Poppy shook her head. "No, thanks. Mrs. Fangtooth said there was a princess in the park, and I want to meet her. And I can't leave Sam."

"What does the princess look like?" Rosie asked.

"I have no idea," Poppy told her. "But I bet she would wear a crown, right?"

Poppy and her friends looked around. No one was wearing a

crown, but maybe princesses didn't wear glittery treasures to the park. If Poppy were a princess, she would wear a crown every day. She'd even wear it in the bathtub.

"If I were a princess, I'd wear a **sparkly** dress. I'd never take it off!" Aqua said loudly. Poppy laughed, but wherever she looked, she didn't see anyone wearing a fancy dress.

"And don't princesses have to wave to people all the time?" Rosie asked.

Freddie frowned. "That sounds boring. And I sure don't see anyone waving right now."

"Maybe she already left," Aqua said.

Had Poppy missed her?

Maybe Mrs. Fangtooth was wrong. Maybe the princess hadn't come to the park after all.

Are You a Princess?

"Why would you want to meet a princess anyway?" Rosie asked.

"I've heard she likes animals," Freddie said.

"Ooh," Aqua squealed. She

loved animals too, dolphins most of all.

"She's also a good singer," Freddie told them.

Rosie shouted as she twirled around on her tail, **"I love to sing!"**

Poppy stared at Freddie. "How do you know so much about the princess, anyway?" she asked.

Freddie held up some mud on a stick. **"It's a mud-pop!"**

"Freddie?" Rosie asked. "It

does sound like you know the princess. Do you?"

All three mergirls circled around him.

"No, but my mom owns the newspaper. She tells me lots of fun facts," Freddie said.

"So, there *really* is a princess here in Trident City?" Poppy asked.

"Yes! There is," Freddie said before turning away to play with Sam and Shelly.

Poppy smiled at Aqua, who smiled at Rosie.

"You know what we need to do?" Poppy cried.

"We need to find the princess!"

Aqua and Rosie sang. "Let's go!"

Poppy pointed to a mergirl in a pink **frilly** dress. "She could be a princess."

Poppy stopped and floated over to her muddy brother. "Sam, you have to come with us."

"No, Poppy, no! We're making something super!" Sam grinned as he, Freddie, and Shelly patted mounds of mud into a big blob.

"Don't worry, Poppy. I'll stay with Sam," Freddie told her.

Poppy lit up. "Thanks so much.

Do you promise to stay with Freddie?" she asked Sam.

Sam nodded. **"I promise!"**

Then Shelly stopped build-

ing the slimy blob. Her long red hair had mud splattered all over it. She even had a spot on her nose. She was muddier than Sam. "I'll stay too. We are making an amazing creation."

"Thanks, Shelly. We'll see you later," Poppy said.

Poppy, Aqua, and Rosie swam toward the mergirl floating beside a **kelp** field. Her pink dress had lots of ruffles. A long necklace of sparkling white pearls hung around her neck. She even had a gold tail.

Aqua grinned. "That *has* to be her.

Suddenly Poppy was afraid. "Maybe we shouldn't bother her."

"Of course we should!"

Rosie said. Aqua and Rosie raced toward the mergirl. Poppy took a deep breath and followed. She crossed her fingers that the princess wouldn't be mad.

"We hope you don't mind us asking," Aqua said shyly, "but are you a princess?"

The mergirl spun around and smiled. "No, I'm not. But what makes you think I am?"

"You are wearing a grand

dress," Rosie told her.

"And you have a gold tail," Aqua added.

Poppy pointed to the mergirl's necklace. "You have pearls. Don't princesses have lots of **jewelry**?"

The mergirl shook her head. "Clothes don't make you a princess."

The friends thanked her and swam away.

"What about her?" Aqua

nodded to a mergirl with a tail of bright green with a star on it.

"**Oooh,**" Rosie squealed. "I bet she's the princess."

"Let's find out," Poppy cried. But when they asked her, the mergirl only laughed at them.

Aqua frowned as they swam away. "I don't think there's a princess here after all."

"Wait a minute," Poppy said. "What about her?"

The friends couldn't believe their eyes. A mermaid twisted

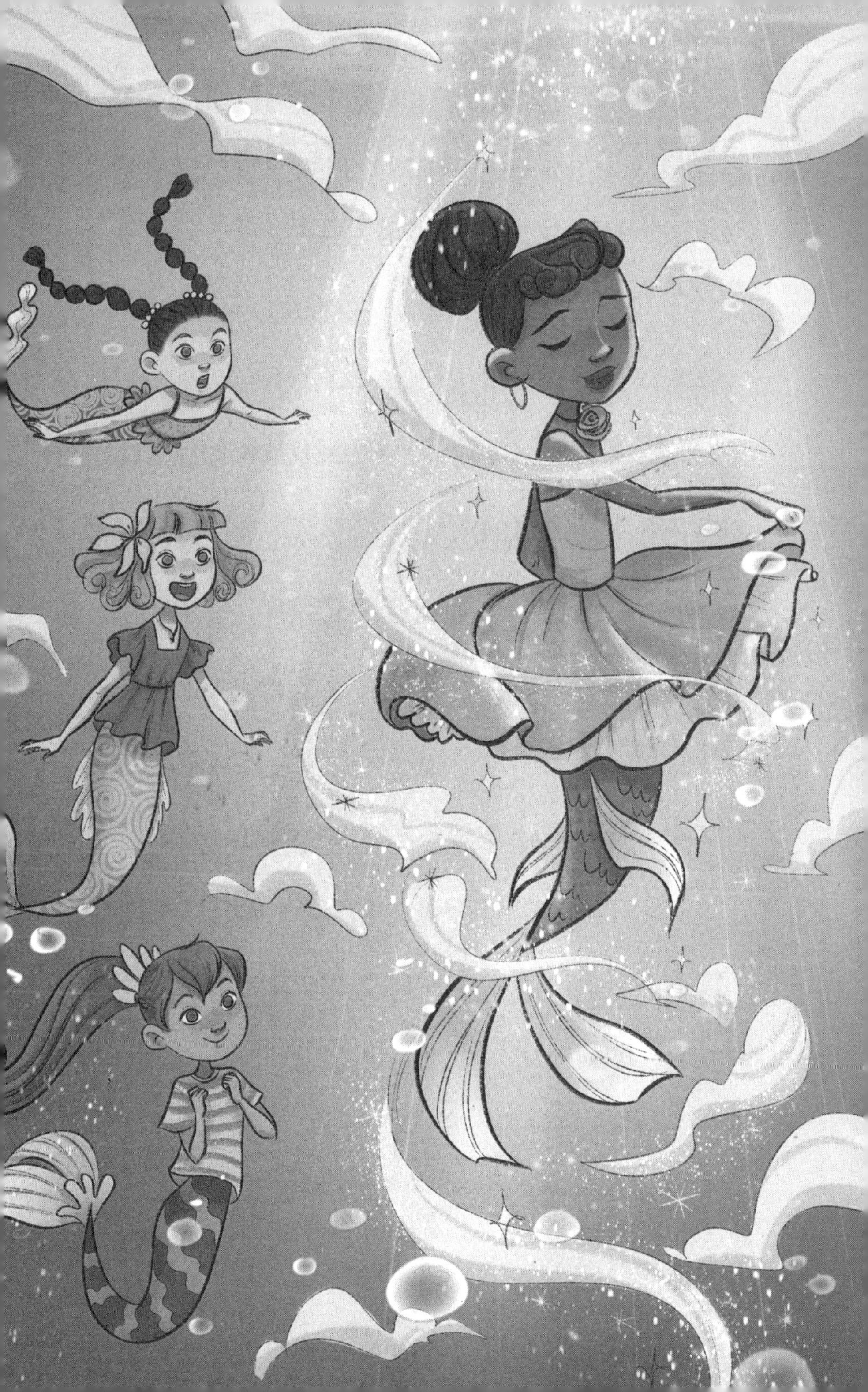

and twirled in an incredible flip.

"Only a princess could do that!" Aqua announced. The three of them rushed over to the mergirl as she landed **gracefully** on the ocean bottom.

"Are you a princess?" Rosie blurted out.

"What are you talking about?" the mergirl asked.

"The librarian, Mrs. Fangtooth, told me that a princess was in the park today," Poppy told her. "Are *you* the princess?"

"No, I'm not. I just like doing flips. And I practice all the time."

"You're really a super star," Aqua said.

"Good luck finding the princess!" the mergirl said as the girls floated away.

As they swam, Poppy thought about the different mergirls they had met.

"Maybe a princess isn't about being beautiful, wearing sparkly clothes and jewelry, flipping through the water, or even having a gold tail, or one with a star on it," she said.

"Then what should a princess be?" Rosie asked.

Princess in the Park

"That's a good question, Rosie. I really don't know what a princess should be like," Poppy told her. "But I need to check on Sam now."

The mergirls floated slowly

through the park over to Sam. When he spotted his sister, he gave Poppy a huge hug.

She was left with a giant glob of mud on her shirt.

"Oh, Sam!" she cried out. "I was trying to stay clean to meet the princess. But I guess that really doesn't matter now."

Sam hung his head. "I'm sorry, Poppy. But the princess told me she likes mud . . . a lot."

Poppy tried to clean off her shirt. "What are you talking about, Sam? We looked all over the park, and we couldn't find a princess anywhere."

"I did meet the princess. Really, Poppy. And she was so nice. We even built something **massive** together." Sam pulled Poppy toward a group of merkids.

"Did all these kids help you?" Aqua asked.

"We worked together, but the princess was the **leader**," he answered.

Sam pointed to the group of kids. Poppy had never seen so much dirt!

Grimy hair stuck up in all directions.

Muck splattered their clothes.

Hands and tails were coated in slime.

They looked like mud monsters. And not one of them looked like a princess!

"That can't be right," Poppy said. "I'm sure a princess isn't messy."

Aqua tapped Sam's shoulder. "Where is she, Sam?" she asked.

"Gee, I don't see her anywhere," he answered.

Poppy felt like crying. They were too late.

Biggest and Best

But then Sam grinned. "Oh wait! There she is."

Poppy swirled around.

A slimy mermaid gave a pat to the gigantic muddy tower. **It was Shelly!**

Her long red hair flowed all around her, and was mud covered. Only one fin of her blue tail stuck out of the mud puddle. She didn't seem to care one bit.

She laughed and added more mud to their huge creation. It

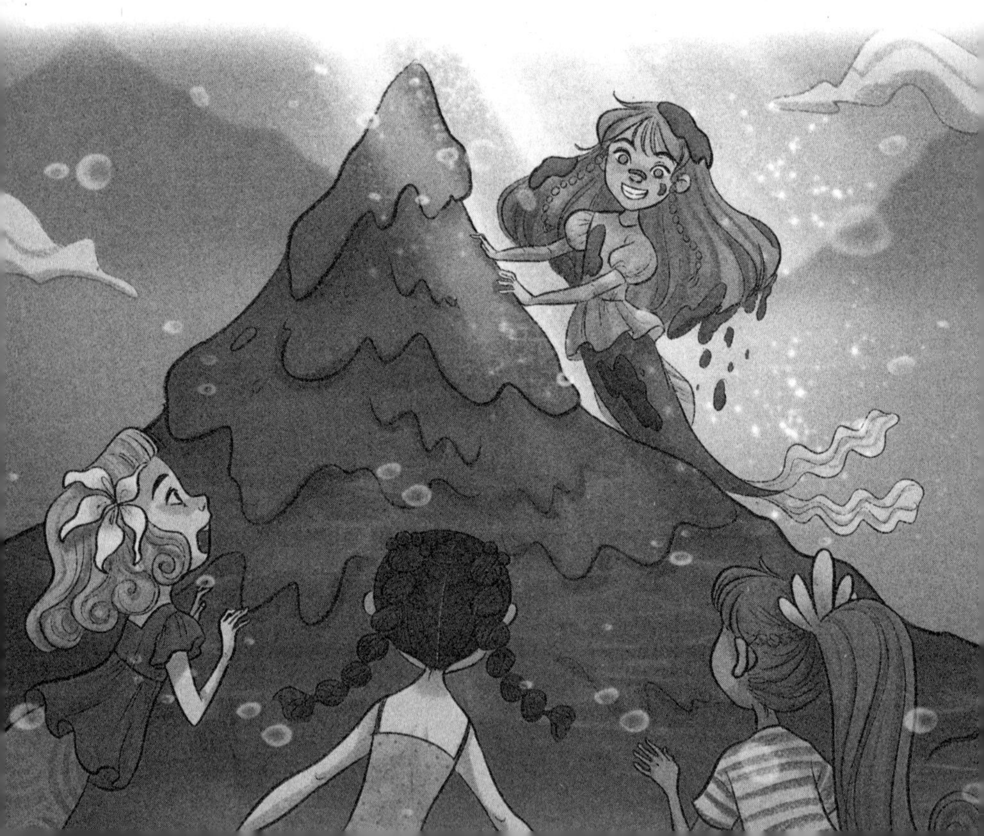

might have started out as a mud pie, but now it was something completely different.

"Look what we made!" Sam called to his big sister.

"Wow, Sam. It's so cool," Poppy said. But she wasn't sure what it was.

Rosie swam over to Shelly. "Are you really a princess?" she asked.

Poppy was sure that Sam was **mistaken**. Shelly couldn't be. She wasn't wearing a crown or a frilly dress. Or jewelry or a star. She definitely wasn't doing flips.

Shelly wiped a mucky hand on her shirt. "I really am. I'm Princess Shelly of the Western Oceans. My great-aunt is Queen Edwina."

"You can't be," Poppy said. She couldn't believe it!

"I am," Shelly answered. She grinned with muddy lips.

Rosie tapped Poppy on the back. "Are we supposed to **curtsy**?" she asked.

Princess Shelly held up a handful of mud.

"That's very kind of you. But there is no need to curtsy. But..." She paused, smiling slyly. "Would you like to help and get dirty? We're almost done."

"What are you making?" Aqua said.

"Can't you tell?" Freddie answered.

Poppy giggled. She had finally figured it out. "What else would a princess make in the mud? It's a mud castle!"

Poppy, Rosie, Aqua, Freddie,

Sam, and Princess Shelly worked as a team. Before long they had helped build the biggest, best mud castle ever.

They were dirty, but no one was muddier than the princess.

"I thought princesses would never play in the mud," Poppy told Shelly.

Shelly shrugged. "Princesses are like all people. Some are tall. Some are short. Some like school. Some don't," she said.

Some like to wear pretty dresses. Some don't. Some like to sing. Some don't."

Poppy nodded. "But the best princesses are nice."

Shelly winked. "I think so too! Come on, let's play with our mud castle."

"It's fin-tastic!" yelled Sam.

And it was.

Word List

bouquet (boh•KAY): Flowers picked and fixed together in a bunch

coated (KOH•ted): Covered with a layer of something

crowd (KRAOOD): A large group of people

curtsy (KURT•see): Bend the knees to show respect

enchanting (en•CHAN•ting): Powerfully pleasing

frilly (FRIH•lee): Decorated with a fancy ruffle

gracefully (GRAYS•fuh•lee): In a fine manner

jewelry (JOO•uhl•ree): Rings, necklaces, earrings, and bracelets

kelp (KELP): A type of plant that grows in the sea

leader (LEE•durr): The person in charge

massive (MA•sihv): Bulky or heavy

mistaken (muh•STAY•kuhn): Wrong

neighbor (NAY•burr): One living near another

plunked (PLUNKT): Dropped suddenly

sparkly (SPAWR•kuh•lee): Reflecting bright points of light

squirted (SKWER•ted): Came forth in a quick spurt

suspected (suh•SPEK•ted): Imagined to be likely

tempted (TEMP•ted): Urged to do something

Questions

1. Why was Poppy surprised when she found the princess?
2. Has anyone ever surprised you by being different than you thought they would be? If so, how did you react?
3. What is the most important thing for a princess, wearing pretty clothes or being a leader? Give a reason for your answer.

4. Would you like to be a princess? Why or why not?
5. If you were a princess, what would you do? How would you be a leader and help other people?